LOOK OUT FOR THE NEXT

NELLY THE MONSTER SITTER

ADVENTURE

COMING SOON

WHAT THEY'RE SAYING ABOUT

*'Once I had started this book
I didn't want to leave it.'*
Becky, age 11

'I love all the different monsters!'
Dylan, age 8

'I would give this book 10 out of 10!'
Suzi, age 8

*'Nelly's adventures make you laugh
and her ways of coping with the monsters
are very funny.'*
Niamh, age 10

*'I enjoyed it so much I have passed it on to
my friend … the funny monster names
made me laugh out loud.'*
Alice, age 9

'It had me laughing from start to finish.'
Katie, age 9

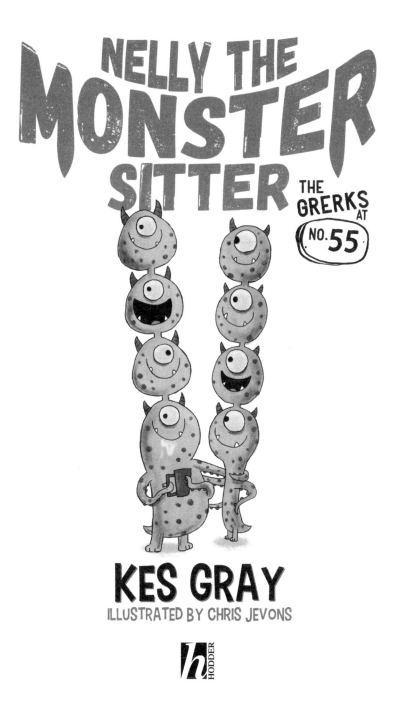

NELLY THE MONSTER SITTER

THE GRERKS AT NO. 55

KES GRAY

ILLUSTRATED BY CHRIS JEVONS

HODDER CHILDREN'S BOOKS

First published in Great Britain in 2018 by Hodder and Stoughton
A version of this story was published in Great Britain
in 2005 by Hodder Children's Books

1 3 5 7 9 10 8 6 4 2

A CIP catalogue record for this book
is available from the British Library.

ISBN 978 1 444 94439 6

Printed and bound in great Britain by Clays Ltd, Elcograf S.p.A.

The paper and board used in this book
are made from wood from responsible sources.

MIX
Paper from
responsible sources
FSC® C104740

Hodder Children's Books
An imprint of
Hachette Children's Group
Part of Hodder and Stoughton
Carmelite House
50 Victoria Embankment
London EC4Y 0DZ

An Hachette UK Company
www.hachette.co.uk

www.hachettechildrens.co.uk

TO THE TILLINGHASTS
AT NUMBER TWO

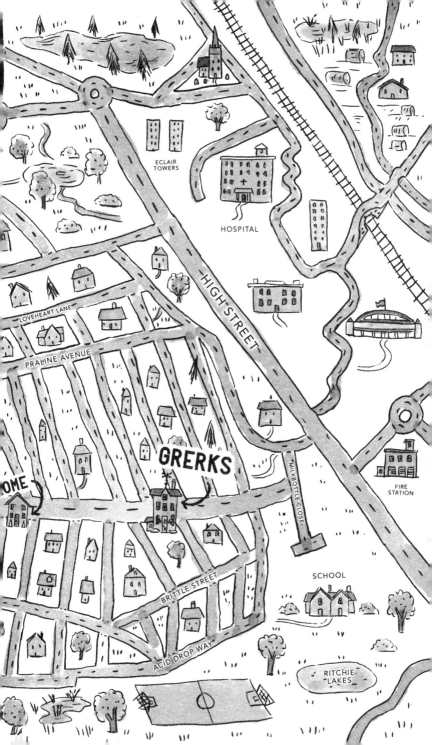

'If monsters are real, how come I've never seen one?' said Nelly.

'Because they never go out,' said her dad.

'Why don't monsters ever go out?' said Nelly.

'Because they can never get a babysitter,' said her dad.

Nelly thought about it. Her mum and dad never went out unless they could get a babysitter. Why should monsters be any different?

'Then I shall become Nelly the Monster Sitter!' smiled Nelly.

CHAPTER 1

There were four drawers in Petronella Morton's
bedside cabinet. One was extra special with
a secret hidden inside, three were as dull as
school. Nelly, as she much preferred to be
called, knelt down excitedly in front of drawer
number four and slowly eased it open.

A spark ignited in both eyes as her fingers
withdrew the secret from its hiding place.
She laid it on her lap, paused for a moment
and then stroked it lovingly with the tips of
her fingers.

It was a lime-green hot water bottle. *Made in Taiwan. Do not overfill.*

Nelly cradled it in her lap for a moment and then opened the flat end of the water bottle like a pitta bread. Unbeknown to her mum she had changed the use of the water bottle entirely by slicing open the widest end with a craft knife.

Nelly slipped her fingers into the secret cavity and pulled out her pride and joy. It was an A4 pad, spiral-bound. The plain red cover had been transformed by the addition of a large title handwritten with silver and gold glitter pens: *Nelly the Monster Sitter's Secret Monster-Sitting Notebook* (in gold) – *KEEP OUT ASTI, OR ELSE* (double underlined in silver, three exclamation marks!!!).

Nelly's secret monster-sitting notebook was for her eyes only. Not that she was a secretive

girl; she had simply decided that most of the things that she saw when she went monster sitting were best kept to herself. You know: gunky, slimy, spiky stuff that other people can find scary or hair-raising.

Monster sitting was Nelly's special thing. None of her friends would ever dare babysit for a family of monsters, or even knock on a monster's front door. Just about everyone Nelly knew, including her twin sister Astilbe (or Asti, as she much preferred to be called), thought that monsters were freaks to be avoided rather than neighbours to be embraced.

But then, Nelly wasn't like most other children. Or most other people, for that matter.

She was an eleven-year-old girl with a heart the size of an air balloon and nerves as steady as an oil rig.

Thankfully for Nelly, her mum and dad were monster-friendly too.

From day one, they had been totally fine
with Nelly's idea of helping monsters to get out
of the house a little bit more. Nelly's dad was of
the mind that babysitting for monsters would
be 'educational'. Nelly's mum was hoping
it might help Nelly with her table manners.
For sure, Nelly was lucky to have parents like
Clifford and Yvonne Morton.

With a glance at the door of her bedroom Nelly opened her secret notebook and flicked randomly through some of the pages. Each was headed neatly in her own handwriting with the name of a monster:

'HOJPOGS', 'WIZZILS', 'GLOOBLES' …

… none were the page she was looking for.

Where's the next blank one? she thought, continuing to flick before stopping with a smile.

Nelly liked the blank pages in her notebook best of all, because for her a blank page was a new monster-sitting adventure waiting to happen. And on this occasion, a new colour gel pen to try out.

Grerks

'GRERKS' she wrote, in her very neatest and newest purple at the very top of the page. Three dots … she added before returning her diary to its water bottle. (Three dots meaning, 'More info later'.)

Nelly was a monster sitter in demand. She had a visit to the Grerks pencilled in to her diary for later that evening, and had never in her entire life seen a Grerk before. Only when she returned after her adventure would her new purple gel pen be able to complete the story.

She knew what Grerks sounded like over the telephone, although she had originally mistaken their squeaking squawks for a Squiddl's. But as for appearances ... were they scaly, were they spiky or slimy or furry? For Nelly, half the fun was guessing, the other half was finding out.

The Grerks at number 55 had asked Nelly if she could monster sit from six o'clock until eight o'clock that evening. It was twenty to six already and she hadn't even had her dinner yet. Not that dinner was ever very much to look forward to in Nelly's house, her parents being less than blessed in the kitchen department.

With another glance at her bedroom door Nelly slipped her water bottle carefully back into place and closed the drawer. She was expecting someone, and that someone was about to arrive.

'Open this door or I'll tell Mum!' squealed
her sister, throttling the handle of Nelly's
bedroom door with a twist, a rattle and a
shake. 'Why have you locked it?'

'So Barbies can't get in,' shouted Nelly, who most days of the week didn't get on with her sister much, and the other days of the week didn't get on with her at all.

'Let me in now or I'll tell Mum and Dad!' shouted Asti.

Nelly rose calmly from her bed and opened the door of her wardrobe instead. It was time to get dressed to go monster sitting, not time to talk to an annoying sister with anger management issues.

'Go away, I'm getting dressed,' Nelly shouted, taking out her favourite, coolest sweatshirt and laying it on the bed.

Nelly loved her monster-sitting sweatshirt. It was purple with an orange trim and in big swirly silver letters it had the word *sardine* transfer-printed across the chest.

No one (including Nelly) understood exactly why the word *sardine* had been printed on to the sweatshirt. But that was precisely why

Nelly liked it. Because it was different.

'Almost ready,' she whispered to herself,
turning away from her wardrobe mirror,
opening the door of her bedroom and barging
past her sister.

'Freak lover,' said Asti.

'Bog tentacle,' said Nelly.

Asti placed her hands on her hips and glared at the back of Nelly's purple sweatshirt as it breezed past her in the direction of the stairs. She had never been as quick-thinking as Nelly and needed time to upgrade her next insult. The words *Smelly, Freako* and *Weirdo* bandied about in her brain, but by the time she had hit

BOG TENTACLE

upon 'Gunge Lover',
Nelly had disappeared
from view.

As usual Nelly was ten steps ahead of
her sister. She bounced down the stairs and
wheeled towards the kitchen in the faint hope
that tea might be ready and waiting for her
on the table.

But as usual, a bottle of tomato sauce was the only thing on offer.

Mealtime had never been a simple affair in Nelly's house. Her mum was a vegetarian, her dad was descended from a lion, her sister was a

fusspot and Nelly didn't like carrots. Actually, she secretly didn't mind carrots but seeing as everyone else in her family was so picky about what they ate, she had decided to have a mealtime no-no of her own.

With expectations of a slap-up dinner low, Nelly walked into the kitchen and found her mum staring at the kitchen counter trying to work out what she could cook for everyone that would involve the minimum amount of effort and the least amount of washing up.

'Mum,' said Nelly, 'is dinner ready, 'cos I'm monster sitting the Grerks at six and I need to leave at ten to.'

Nelly's mum stared blankly at the ingredients in front of her, replacing the chicken nuggets with a frozen herring and then swapping a tin of macaroni cheese for three large sticks of celery and an avocado.

'I do wish you liked carrots, Nelly, it would make life so much easier,' she sighed.

'Why don't we have a takeaway?' suggested Nelly, sensing an opportunity to avoid her mum's cooking altogether.

Nelly's mum threw her arms up into the air. 'Brilliant idea!' she said, sweeping the avocado and celery back into the vegetable rack and tossing an assortment of tins back into the carousel. 'A pizza it is!'

'Can you order it for eight o'clock?' asked Nelly. 'I'll be back just after.'

'Brilliant brilliant!' said Nelly's mum, bending the herring back into an overly full compartment of the freezer. 'I'll go and put my feet up for a couple of hours. I could do with a break. I wonder what's on telly?'

'The usual Saturday night rubbish,' said Nelly's dad, limping into the kitchen from the garden. 'It's always rubbish telly on a Saturday.'

All eyes switched to Clifford.

'Why are you sucking your thumb, Dad??' asked Nelly.

'Snowball,' he winced.

'You've been poking your fingers through the rabbit cage again, haven't you?' said her mum. 'You know Snowball only likes Nelly.'

It was true. The Morton family rabbit was a one-person rabbit. As white as snow and as fluffy as thistledown, he looked as cutesy wutesy as a bunnykins could look, but lurking beneath that little twitchy nose and those soft whiskers was a killerkins: two needle-sharp teeth with enough strength to crunch into a steel carrot and meet in the middle.

Nelly had never been sure why Snowball
had singled her out as his one true friend in the
world, but hey, if it made Asti jealous it had to
be a good thing.

Nelly's dad threw a pitiful glance at his wife

and then limped to the kitchen sink.

(Nelly's dad always limped when he was looking for sympathy.)

'Why are you limping again?' asked Nelly's mum. 'Next you'll be telling me the rabbit tripped you up as well!'

'Maybe Snowball picked Dad up, swung him round his head and body-slammed him on to the patio!' laughed Nelly.

Nelly's dad sighed. If he was looking for sympathy then he was most certainly in the wrong room at the wrong time with the wrong people.

Things tipped slightly more in his favour with the arrival of Asti.

'Ooh you poor love!' she cooed, seeing that her dad was in mild distress and seizing the opportunity to gain some major brownie points.

Nelly groaned inwardly as her sister ran across the kitchen and threw her arms around her dad's waist.

'Ooh that's nasty, is it deep?' she gushed. 'How did it happen?'

'Snowball,' gasped her dad bravely.

'I hate that rabbit,' snapped Asti angrily. 'We should have it put down before someone gets killed.'

Nelly looked at her mum. Nelly's mum looked at Nelly's dad. Everyone looked at Asti. For a girl with very little imagination she had certainly surpassed herself this time.

Sensing she might have overstepped the mark, Asti backtracked fast.

'OK, not killed exactly, but what if
Snowball bit someone and they caught
some hideous rabbit disease from his
teeth or his rabbit dribble or something?
What then?'

No one was convinced.

'Oh, I give up!' sighed Asti, glaring at her dad and then flouncing back upstairs to put on some more cherry lip-gloss. 'It's only a nip and anyway you should be on my side because I was on yours.'

Nelly looked at her watch and sidled towards the front door. It was time to escape in the direction of her next monster-sitting adventure.

'I'll be back just after eight,' she said, writing the Grerks' telephone number and house number on a pink Post-it note and sticking it on the hall mirror by the front door.

'Can I have an American Hot with extra hot chillies please,' she shouted, 'and some garlic bread to ward off evil Astis!'

'Stop winding your sister up,' growled her mum. 'And don't forget to leave the Grerks' telephone num—'

'I've stuck it in the usual place,' said Nelly, grabbing her coat from its hook and opening the front door.

'I hope some disgusting twelve-headed swamp monster eats you,' cackled Asti from the top of the stairs.

'They always lose their appetite once I've told them about you,' smiled Nelly.

Asti wavered, stung by a quick-fire Nellyism. But before she had time to even raise her foot to stamp it, Nelly had skipped triumphantly into the front garden and closed the door.

'Gunge lover!' shouted Asti, to no one but the letter box. 'Ooohh, I can't stand that girl!'

CHAPTER 2

For Nelly, monster sitting was a chance to be exactly like the sweatshirt: different. Especially different from her sister Asti.

Life can be so samey when you're an identical twin. Everyone expects you to be one half of the same person, to wear the same clothes, to do the same things, to feel the same way. Everyone jumps to the same samey conclusions about you both – and yet Nelly wasn't like Asti at all. OK, she and Asti were similarish to look at but in every other way they were as different as no and yes.

Nelly wasn't afraid of monsters. Asti was.
Nelly thought monsters were lovely. Asti didn't.
Nelly didn't mind shaking a seven-fingered
paw. Asti did. Nelly was happy to play leapfrog
with a four-foot-tall amphibious creature
with long dangly tentacles and suckers on its
foreheads. Asti wasn't.

Being a monster sitter had given Nelly
the chance to prove just how unidentical an
identical twin could be.

The street that Nelly lived in was a very long street, busy with traffic during the early and late parts of the day but quieter during the afternoon hours.

Nelly looked at her watch. She was only three minutes from the Grerks' front door and counting down to 'ding dong' time. (Assuming the Grerks' doorbell went 'ding dong'.)

Twelve houses further down Sweetman Street, she began to take careful notice of the house numbers that were approaching.

Number 55 was an odd number. That meant that on this particular monster visit, there would be no need for her to cross the road. With a tingle of excitement she quickened her step and began tapping the front gates with her fingers as she passed them.

'Scaly, four ears and a giant head. I bet that's what a Grerk looks like … or maybe two heads,' she mused.

Her eyes strimmed across the top of a line of privet hedging and then darted diagonally across, trying to glean a clue from the colour of the front door.

'63 … 61 … 59 … 57 … 55,' she counted. 'Four heads!' she smiled. 'A purple front door usually means four heads!'

As soon as she arrived at the front gate of number 55, Nelly stopped, adjusted her scrunchie and then ironed her sweatshirt with the palms of her hands. First impressions were very important to her. So was being on time.

She looked at her watch. It was 5.59 and forty-seven seconds. She composed herself for

thirteen seconds, walked jauntily down the
path to the purple front door and pressed the
custard-yellow doorbell hard with her finger.

The doorbell *'dong dinged'* loudly.

'Definitely four heads,' she smiled to herself.
'Or I'm a Grimp's hairdo!'

CHAPTER 3

The moment Nelly's finger released the doorbell a fierce wolfish growl erupted in the hallway on the other side of the door. *Interesting!* she thought, staring at the purple high-gloss door and bravely standing her ground.

SQUEAKS and SQUAWKS

were approaching now.

'Here goes,' she smiled, as the door of number 55 opened slowly with a creak.

The instant the door opened, Nelly's eyes sky-scrapered upwards. A pink onion-sized eye was staring inquisitively down at her from a green cabbage-sized head.

Nelly's eyes lowered and were met by a second head. She lowered her sights again and began counting under her breath. One two three four green heads were perched like traffic lights one on top of the other, each with a pink onion eye swivelling erratically inside its socket.

With a squeaking squawk, each of the four mouths spoke together.

'Are you Nelly the Monster Sitter?'

'That's me!' smiled Nelly, jumping backwards down the path as a fifth head with two orange dangly tongues suddenly appeared from the bottom of the door and lunged in the direction of her knees. 'You must be the Grerks! Very pleased to meet you!'

The Grerks were clearly as pleased to meet Nelly as Nelly was to meet them. Especially head number five. Nelly stood back for a moment as the four heads at the top tried to control the one head at the bottom.

In and out the heads popped. Up and down the heads bobbed. Only when the door opened for a third time did it swing back all the way.

Wow, thought Nelly, smiling politely in as many different directions as she could. *Nine heads now!*

Not one, but two large green reptilian monsters were now standing in the hallway. One of them was now cradling a smaller and considerably wriggly monster in its arms.

'We're so sorry about that, Nelly,' said the Grerk that still had all three of its tentacles dangling free. 'We hope he didn't frighten you. He gets so excited when he sees strangers. Please, let us introduce ourselves. My name is Scroot, this is my wife Pummice and this is our little handful, Glug!'

Nelly stepped forward and held out her hand. 'I'm very pleased to meet you,' she said, waiting politely for an invitation to enter the house.

'Do come in, do come in!' beckoned Scroot. 'Please make yourself at home.'

Nelly stepped excitedly into the Grerks'
hallway and bumped immediately into a
pasting table piled high with rolls of purple
hairy wallpaper.

'Mind the table. And the bucket!' squawked
Pummice, leading Nelly down the hallway.
'We're in the middle of redecorating!'

In all the monster homes she'd visited Nelly had never seen hairy wallpaper before. 'You certainly are!' she laughed, running her fingers lightly across a yet-to-be pasted roll.

'Don't touch the Monsta-Paste either,' squeaked Scroot. 'It will stick you to the wall!'

'Perhaps you could tell me where to buy it!' laughed Nelly, peering into a large turquoise bucket full to the brim with a pea-green slop. 'I'm actually thinking of having a change-around in my bedroom too!'

'Well, if you need any wallpaper we've got lots of rolls left over!' laughed Scroot.

'I don't think I could hang wallpaper that heavy,' said Nelly, suspecting that one roll alone probably had the weight of a small Persian rug.

'Quick-drying Monsta-Paste will stick anything,' squeaked Pummice, pointing back at the bucket.

'Make sure you have a big sticky brush though!' squawked Scroot.

Nelly stepped gingerly past the Monsta-Paste and followed the Grerks to the lounge.

'We're undecided what colour scheme to go for in here,' squawked Scroot, stepping through the doorway and waving his tentacles in all directions at once.

Nelly scanned the room. Tins of yellow and black spotty paint were piled up by the window, green and purple swatches were daubed on to the bare walls. The window frames had been sploshed with blue and green stripes and three grades of hairy wallpaper had been slapped on to the wall behind the sofa. At least, Nelly assumed it was a sofa. It was hard to tell because all the furniture in the room was wrapped up in silver foil.

'It protects the fabric,' said Pummice, pre-empting Nelly's question. 'We don't want to redecorate our sofas too!'

Nelly sat down with a soft aluminium crunch and stared at the walls.

'We're not sure whether to go hairy or slimy in here,' said Scroot, frowning at the walls with all four eyebrows.

'Maybe a break from decorating will give you a chance to clear your heads,' smiled Nelly.

'All eight of them!' chuckled Pummice. 'And that's precisely why you are here!'

'It's a pleasure to be here!' said Nelly, holding out her arms. 'Are you going to introduce me to Glug properly?'

'I'm not sure you should try and hold him though, he's very wriggly!'

'And waggy,' said Nelly, staring at a blur of wagging tails.

Glug was big for a baby, about the size of a

goat. But that wasn't all. He looked so different to Pummice and Scroot it wasn't true. For a start he most definitely did not have four heads. He had one head with two long orange tongues that flopped out either side of a broad sharp-toothed mouth. He had a long hairy coat and sat low and squat like a bow-legged tortoise. He had five tails that wouldn't stop wagging and six legs that wouldn't stop hopping. Even to the most untrained of monster-sitting eyes, the dissimilarity between Glug and his parents was quite striking.

'Say hello to Nelly, Glug,' said Pummice. 'NICELY I mean, say hello NICELY to Nelly.'

Nelly watched as Pummice lowered Glug gently down on the floor and then braced herself as his two orange tongues came slobbering and slavering her way.

'Isn't he ugliful!' squeaked Pummice, kissing Glug tenderly on the nose with her third head.

'He likes you!' squealed Scroot. 'Look, I've never seen his tails wag so fast!'

Nelly slid off the armchair on to her knees, pursed her lips and welcomed Glug with open arms.

Boy could he lick. Whichever way Nelly turned her head a tongue was waiting to greet her.

'If you don't mind me saying,' she gasped between slurps, 'he doesn't look very much like you!'

Pummice and Scroot turned and blinked softly at one another as one by one by one by one, their thin reptilian mouths cracked open with uncontrollable laughter.

'Of course he doesn't look like us, Nelly!

Glug isn't a Grerk, he's a gog! Don't you have gogs at home, Nelly?'

Nelly grimaced as Glug used his tongue like a pasting brush to slap saliva across her ear and then giggled as she realised her mistake.

'We have *dogs*, not gogs!' blurted Nelly, deciding that she'd had quite enough Glug slobber for one visit. 'But not as licky as this!'

Scroot leant forward on the sofa and clapped his tentacles loudly.

'NICELY Glug, Mummy said NICELY!'

'It's OK!' laughed Nelly, climbing to her feet and easing herself back on to the sofa. 'He's only being friendly,' she chuckled, patting Glug on the top of his head and then wiping her face with her sleeve.

Sensing that fuss time was over, Glug turned

his attentions elsewhere, gatoring across the floor, jumping back into Pummice's lap and flipping over expectantly on to his back. 'He loves having his tummy tickled,' said Pummice, obliging with all three tentacles. 'He's a right little tickletum, is Gluggy!'

'He's no ordinary gog either, Nelly,' boasted Scroot. 'Glug is a Pedigree Best of Breed Golden Revolver. He's been Supreme Ugly Champion of Champions at Grunts for the last three years running!'

'And tomorrow you're going to win again, aren't you, Gluggy-wug!' said Pummice, giving the scales on Glug's tum an extra scratch. 'We're going to buy our Gluggy-wuggy a beautiful new bow and a sparkling new collar especially for tomorrow's show, aren't we?'

Nelly smiled uncertainly. She had never babysat a monster pet before. She knew all too well that surprises always lurked behind a monster's front door, but she had never before given a moment's thought to gog sitting.

'We really should be off, Nelly,' squawked

Pummice, lowering Glug to the floor, standing up and then brushing herself down with every available tentacle, 'before the late-night shopping ends.'

'We have to buy some more alligator chunks too,' added Scroot. 'Would it be all right if we leave you a couple of instructions before we go?'

Nelly stood up and followed Pummice and Scroot into the kitchen.

'Alligator chunks?' she frowned. 'Did Scroot actually just say alligator chunks?'

'Glug loves alligator chunks!' squeaked Pummice, scanning the spotlessly clean surfaces of the pink and lime-green stripy kitchen units.

Scroot opened a kitchen cupboard door, reached up high with a tentacle and slapped some suckers around a large tin.

A very large tin actually, about the size of a
five-litre paint pot.

'Last one!' Scroot squawked, gripping the
tin like a boa constrictor and placing it on

the counter with ease. 'We've tried him on rat chunks, bat chunks, snake chunks, tarantula chunks and octopus chunks, but alligator is definitely his favourite!'

'Really?' gasped Nelly, ungluing her eyes from the tin and lifting them in the direction of Pummice.

'It's very important that you give Glug his dinner at seven o'clock,' squeaked Pummice, tapping Nelly on the shoulder with one tentacle. 'Champion Show gogs have a very carefully controlled dietary routine. Remember Nelly, seven o'clock. No later, no sooner.'

Nelly looked down at Glug, who was now panting excitedly by her feet.

'I promise I'll remember.' Nelly nodded dutifully. 'Can you leave me out a tin opener please, so that I can open the can?'

'Of course,' squeaked Pummice, plunging her tentacles into a kitchen drawer and placing the biggest tin opener Nelly had ever seen on the counter.

'Thank you!' said Nelly. 'Do I give him the whole tin?'

'No, only the alligator chunks inside,' squawked Scroot.

'Golden Revolvers can be very greedy, but we never let him eat the tin!' nodded Pummice.

That wasn't exactly what I meant, thought Nelly, deciding to smile rather than explain.

'I'm sure he would eat the tin if you let him!' squawked Scroot. 'Especially with those super-sharp sharky-warky teeth!'

Nelly gulped. She quite liked the idea of

monster sitting a gluggy-wuggy gog, but she could have done without the sharky-warky teeth.

'Does Glug like playing games in the garden?' she asked, thinking it might be best to distract those teeth away from the alligator chunks and out into the fresh air.

'He loves chasing gog sticks!' squawked Pummice, throwing open the back door. 'You'll find plenty of gog sticks in the shed, Nelly. Help yourself!'

Nelly gave Glug a pat on the head and then followed Pummice and Scroot out of the kitchen back down the hallway in the direction of the turquoise bucket.

'Mind the Monsta-Paste!' Nelly warned as the Grerks jiggled past the pasting table and approached their front door.

'Oh, that will be set solid by now,' squawked Pummice.

Nelly looked down into the bucket. Pummice was right – the pea-green slop was now a transparent lump of diamond-hard resin.

'Awesome!' she gasped. 'I'd love to pour some on my sister's cornflakes!'

'We didn't know you had a sister!' squeaked Scroot, opening the latch on the front door with his tentacle. 'Is she nice?'

'Not as nice as Glug,' said Nelly. 'Or as pretty.'

'We'll be back by eight o'clock,' squawked Pummice and Scroot, opening the front door and slipping out in a flurry of goodbye tentacles. 'Don't forget, alligator chunks at seven o'clock!'

'I won't forget, I promise,' Nelly replied with a wave.

Nelly carried on waving from the doorstep until Pummice and Scroot were out of sight.

'OK, Gluggy-wug,' she smiled. 'Where are those gog sticks?'

CHAPTER 4

The Grerks' back garden was a garden of contrasts; neat in places (pretty border flowers) and a bombsite in others (courtesy of Glug's digging).

Nelly weaved her way across the lawn and rattled the shed door. It was wooden with an easy-to-lift latch. Nelly gave it a flick with her thumb and craned her neck cautiously inside.

Big problem. The sticks weren't sticks at all: they were branches, tree trunks even, sawn-off telegraph poles possibly. Whatever they were,

they were huge, stacked neatly, planed smooth and in theory ready to throw – provided Nelly could lift one.

Nelly looked back at Glug's five wagging tails. He was very much hoping she could do more than lift one … he wanted her to throw one too. Always up for a challenge, Nelly stepped into the shed.

'Here goes,' she frowned, crouching low like a weight lifter, and then pincering her arms around the full girth of one stick. She was in luck; her fingers just about met in the middle.

The gog stick she had selected was pretty much like every other gog stick in the shed; about five metres long, half a metre thick with a distinct whiff of pine needles.

With a grunt and a gasp, she tugged it, yanked it, finally dislodged it and then began to inch it in the direction of the open shed door.

'Coming, Gluggy,' she gasped, reversing towards the lawn lurch by lurch. 'Good gog,' she gasped, peering over her shoulder to find Glug sitting obediently on the grass behind her.

The stick felt more like the leg of a dinosaur
than a stick you would throw in a park.
Determined not to disappoint those wagging
tails, though, Nelly gritted her teeth and
kept tugging.

Glug was impressed. He had never seen a human bottom reversing towards him before and stared inquisitively at the very strange spectacle. Had it been Pummice or Grerk doing the throwing he would have been in business long before now. A single tentacle could have carried the stick out of the shed with ease and propelled it down the garden like a javelin. Nelly, alas, was a bit lacking in the tentacle department.

With every lurch, her cheeks puffed fuller and fatter. With every gasp, her face flushed redder and hotter. She was a quarter of the way out of the shed now. Only three and a half metres to go.

'Nearly there, Gluggy,' she groaned. 'Good goggy woggy,' she winced. 'Good things come,' she gasped, 'to gogs who wait!'

Glug showed his appreciation with a wag of all five tails and then lowered his chin patiently on to the lawn.

Millimetre by millimetre, groan by groan, Nelly emerged into the early-evening sunshine.

'Ready?' she wheezed, resting the dead weight of the gog stick on her right shoulder for a moment and then psyching herself for stage two – stage two being the throwing bit.

Glug sprang back on to all six feet and began tap dancing on the spot. He was ready, all right. He'd never been more ready in his life.

'Here goes,' she gasped, hoicking the stick off her shoulder and bracing it with the palms of her hands.

At the first sign of upward stick movement

Glug was off, bounding down the lawn, orange tongues flapping. With a howl of excitement he made an ungainly handbrake turn by the patio doors and then waited expectantly for Nelly to throw the stick.

Nelly switched to weightlifter mode again and summoned every last ounce of strength from her wrists, her biceps and her elbows.

'Lift,' she gasped.

Hoick by hoick, brace by brace, she inched the flats of her palms higher and higher up the gog stick until there it finally was, towering precariously above her in a wobbly yet undeniably upright position.

Glug's eyes craned upwards and then bulged large. It was stick time! It was stick time! It might have taken a very long time, but stick time it most certainly was!

'Are you ready to fetch, Gluggy?' gasped Nelly, planting her feet wide as wide as she could to stop the stick falling on top of her.

Glug had been ready for the last twenty minutes and was now yo-yoing on the spot.

Nelly frowned with determination, tensed every sinew in her body and then pushed as hard as she could.

The gog stick, wobbled, wavered, teetered and then toppled like a felled tree to the ground.

'Fetch,' Nelly gasped.

It was the best that she could do.

For a moment Glug seemed confused. This was a game he hadn't played before. He cocked his head to one side, yo-yoed up and down two or three times and then with a wolfish, snarling growl clamped his teeth around the gog stick.

Nelly jumped back in alarm as a whirlwind of tongues, tails and teeth reduced the stick to sawdust.

Yes, sawdust.

Nelly stood motionless on the lawn for a moment and stared down at her feet and legs. Thankfully they were still there, but the gog stick most certainly wasn't.

To her utter amazement Glug had despatched the stick quicker than a buzz saw in a timber yard.

There it was. And now there it wasn't.

And now, judging by the flip-flap and dribble of Glug's two orange tongues, he wanted her to throw ANOTHER stick, all over again!

Nelly knelt down beside the expectant gog and draped her arms wearily around his neck. 'Sorry, Glug,' she panted. 'I'm beat. Please let's play something else.'

With a ruffle of his ears and a tickle of his chest, Nelly twisted her wrist and peered at her watch. The gog stick had taken her more than half an hour to throw, which meant it was already 6.45!

'Alligator chunks. Alligator chunks at seven o'clock,' she reminded herself. 'What can we do for the next fifteen minutes?'

Glug sat obediently at Nelly's feet and waited for her next move.

'No more sticky-wicks for Gluggy-wug,' she said, climbing back to her feet and brushing some grass from her knees. 'I know!' she clapped. 'We'll do commands! If you're a show gog you are bound to be good at commands! Are you good at commands, Gluggy-wuggy? Would you like to do some doggy tricks for Nelly?'

Glug was up for anything and sprang on to all sixes.

Nelly straightened her back, arched her eyebrows and pointed sharply at the ground with her newly elected 'command finger'.

'SIT!' she ordered. 'Sit, Glug, I say!'

Glug double-licked her command finger
and began bouncing around.

He clearly wasn't familiar with the word 'sit'.

Nelly withdrew her finger sharply and stuck
it under her armpit to remove the slobber.

'ROLL OVER!'

she said, electing to use a full, five-fingered
'command hand' this time.

Glug's orange tongues flicked out to greet
her, but this time Nelly was quick to keep her
hand above slobber height.

'Roll over, I said!' frowned Nelly, raising
her hand above Glug's head and repeating
the command with a sequence of barrelling,
turning wrist motions. Glug watched with

interest and then sprang up in an attempt to reward his trainer with another lick.

The words *'roll'* and *'over'* were clearly new to him too.

Nelly withdrew her command hand and scratched her head. If *'sit'* didn't work and *'roll over'* didn't work then she was pretty sure she'd be wasting her time with *'beg'*. And they were the only doggy commands that she knew.

Finding herself a little short on ideas, she looked around the garden. If there had been some balls in the shed she could have tried those.

But there weren't. Was she really going to have to throw another stick?

The very thought of lugging another gog stick out of the shed made her go weak at the knees. Not only that, with only fifteen minutes she'd be lucky to get one as far as the shed door.

'Umm,' she pondered.

'I wonder?' she frowned.

Scroot and Pummice had said Glug was a *Golden Revolver* so that must mean one of two things. Either he fired bullets like a revolver …

Nelly scanned the garden fence and neighbouring windows for bullet holes.

Or maybe … just maybe … could it be? … could it just be?

She decided to chance it.

'REVOLVE!'

she said, circling the air with her command finger.

Glug's ears pricked up instantly and his brown eyes switched to emerald green. Nelly had his full and eager attention now.

'Come on, Gluggy,' she said, repeating the clockwise circling motion with her finger, 'you can do it.'

And do it he could! With his ears pricked high and his emerald eyes gleaming, he revolved his head in a full 360-degree circle!

Nelly's jaw hit the lawn. Emerald-green eyes were one thing, but a revolving head! She really hadn't been expecting that!

'Clever gog,' she gasped, dropping to her knees again and offering up both her cheeks for a double lick.

Glug wagged his tails wildly and treated Nelly to a few more courtesy revolutions.

I wonder if he can revolve in both directions? thought Nelly, raising her hand again and turning her finger anticlockwise.

Her hunch was right. He most certainly could revolve in both directions, only this time, his eyes glowed red instead of green and instead of revolving his head, he revolved his body instead – yes, his whole body, tails, legs, bottom and everything!

'How do you do that?' gasped Nelly. 'No wonder you're a Champion of Champions!'

Glug wagged his tails appreciatively and waited for his next command. But it was time for alligator chunks!

Nelly sprang to her feet.

'Now for your reward!' she laughed, pointing her command finger towards the open kitchen door. 'No more revolving for you, Gluggy, it's din-dins time!'

Glug howled like a wolf, leapt to his feet and began chasing all five tails at once.

He must REALLY LIKE alligator chunks! thought Nelly, hurrying up the garden with Glug nipping playfully at her heels.

When she arrived in the kitchen she found Glug already sitting by his bowl, staring up at the counter. Nelly picked up the can opener and attached it to the lip of the can.

With every twist of the handle, Glug's head swivelled like the light on a light house.

'He DEFINITELY likes alligator chunks!' smiled Nelly, springing back from the dangle of slobber that was hanging from his chin.

With a frown of curiosity she detached the lid from the can and gave it a sniff. It smelt like cheesy feet mixed with bad eggs.

Nelly read the label with a grimace.

Prime chunks of alligator from the smelliest swamps of Florida, squashed into a rank rattlesnake jelly, make GOODGOG alligator chunks the Choice of Champions.

Best before Sep 08 3004.

Good Gog!

ALLIGATOR CHUNKS

Holding her nose, she bent down and picked up Glug's bowl. Holding her breath she placed it on the kitchen counter and turned the can upside down. The contents belched into the bowl like an avalanche of frogspawn. Nelly gagged, placed the bowl on the floor and jumped back.

Glug set upon the bowl like a wolf in a chicken house. In seconds the bowl was empty and being pushed around the kitchen floor by two very licky tongues.

Nelly eased herself up on to the kitchen counter, just in case he fancied her ankles for dessert.

'Did you enjoy that, Gluggy?' she asked, as his tongues finally gave up. Glug wagged his tails appreciatively and then trotted outside into the garden.

'A job well done!' smiled Nelly, jumping down from the kitchen counter, retrieving the bowl and watching from the kitchen window as Glug padded down the lawn and began sniffing round the trunk of a large tree.

Nelly rinsed the bowl under the tap.

She frowned. 'He's not going to? … He is going to!' she gulped.

With a scratch of his coat and a shake of his head, Glug circled the tree three times and then cocked three legs at once. Not one leg. Not two legs, but three legs at once! Without losing his balance!

Nelly watched in amazement and then began to feel a little embarrassed. After all there Glug was, having a very private moment and here she was, gawping at him from the kitchen window.

She did her best to look away, but her curiosity immediately got the better of her. How many sprinkles was it going to be? One, two or three? Her eyes zeroed in on the base of the oak tree but before she could discover the answer, the sound of the front doorbell ping-ponged her head in the opposite direction.

DING

DONG!

Had the Grerks come home early?

Although she doubted it, Nelly had no choice but to forget about sprinkles and answer the door. Placing the bowl on the drainer and wiping her hands on her sweatshirt, she hurried back through the lounge and into the hallway.

When she opened the front door she found not a Grerk, but a rather frail-looking woman in a spotty skirt and grey tweed blouse, smiling at her. She had a wicker basket hooked over her left arm and a small yellow and black striped envelope in her right hand.

'Hello,' said the woman. 'I'm sorry to bother you, but I'm collecting on behalf of the Royal Society for the Prevention of Cruelty to Wasps. I posted an envelope through your letter box earlier in the week.'

Nelly looked down at the envelope that the woman was waving in front of her nose.

'I don't actually live here,' explained Nelly, 'I'm just monster sitting for a couple of hours.'

The charity worker's face pinched with disappointment. Nelly looked into the woman's basket at the one and only sealed envelope that she had managed to collect so far.

'Wait a moment,' said Nelly, her face illuminating, 'I think I know exactly where the Grerks have left their envelope. I'm sure I saw it on the mantelpiece in the lounge!'

The charity worker's face brightened.

'If you'll just excuse me for a moment, I'll go and get it!' said Nelly.

Nelly left the charity worker on the doorstep, threaded her way down the hallway, past the turquoise bucket, past the pasting table and the hairy wallpaper rolls and into the lounge.

She was right. The Grerks had filled and sealed the RSPCW envelope.

The Grerks must love wasps! she thought to herself, taking it from the mantelpiece and feeling the weight of all the coins inside.

'I've found it!' she called out to the charity worker, hurrying back past the dust sheets, paint tins and fabric books. 'It was on the mantelpiece in the loun—?'

As soon as she hit the doorstep, Nelly stopped dead in her tracks. The charity worker was nowhere to be seen.

'Where did she go?' Nelly puzzled, swivelling her head in all directions and doing a passable impression of a Golden Revolver herself.

The answer came from ankle height as a soft whimpering groan drew Nelly's eyes downwards to the garden path. The charity worker was lying there, flat out on her back, and her wicker basket was hanging from a rose bush.

Nelly stared down at her and then gasped.

Plastered across the woman's grey tweed blouse were the six huge pawprints of a rather large gog.

Glug had escaped through the open front door!

'It went that way!' groaned the charity worker, lifting her arm weakly and flopping it in the direction of the garden gate.

Nelly leapt from the step, hurdled the woman's outstretched body and raced to the end of the path. Her head flashed left and right but Glug was nowhere to be seen.

'GLUGGG!'
she shouted.
**'COME
BACCCKKKK!'**
she hollered till her voice was hoarse, but

Glug, the Grunts Supreme Ugly Champion

of Champions show gog, was gone.

'What have I done?' groaned Nelly, trudging miserably back up the path to the house and helping the charity worker to her feet.

'He was only playing,' explained Nelly. 'He's a cutey pie really.'

The charity worker brushed herself down and staggered in the direction of home.

'What are the Grerks going to say?' sighed Nelly, sitting crestfallen on the front step. 'I left the front door wide open. That makes it my fault. What good will a new gog collar and gog bow be if there is no gog to attach them to?'

She checked the time on her phone. It was twenty past seven. In just forty minutes Scroot and Pummice would be walking up the path with a new gog bow and collar in their hands (well, tentacles). It would be bad enough seeing two faces fall when she told them the news but eight heads meant eight faces – that was FOUR times the disappointment.

Whichever way she looked at things, searching for Glug by herself just wasn't an option. She couldn't leave Scroot and Pummice's house and go looking because she had no key to the front door. No key meant no way back in, even if she found Glug. If she went searching and Glug came home while she was out looking for him, there would be no one at home to let him in. Plus, what if she was out looking for him and the Grerks came home early? They would find their house completely empty. What on earth would they think if they opened the door of number 55 and found no Gluggy-wuggy to greet them and no Nelly-welly either? They'd probably think Nelly was a gognapper.

Nelly looked at her phone. She needed help and she needed help fast. She couldn't ask her mum or dad. They'd never be able to get their heads around a gog with a revolving head. And she certainly couldn't trust Asti.

'I know who I'll call!' she smiled. 'GRIT! AND MUMP!'

CHAPTER

5

There are times (like this one) when keeping the company of monsters can have its drawbacks. But there are other times (like this one) when being able to scroll through the friends list on your phone and send a Mayday to a Huffaluk and a Dendrileg can actually be rather handy.

The instant that Grit and Mump heard that Nelly was in trouble, two different doors on the estate crashed open simultaneously.

Mump was the first to hurdle the turquoise
bucket …

… and Grit came thundering up the
hallway of number 55 seconds after.

They found Nelly in the kitchen, anxiously toying with the handle of the can opener.

'He could be anywhere,' she sighed.

Grit patted Nelly's head with all three of his furry paws. 'Don't worry,' he growled. 'He can't have got far.'

'He's got six legs!' said Nelly. 'Imagine how far and how fast we could all run if we had six legs!'

'Wherever he is, we'll find him,' growled Grit.

'I've got an idea,' slurped Mump with a suckery thwuck. 'Why don't we open another couple of tins of alligator chunks? A gog could smell an alligator chunk from ten streets away! If that doesn't attract him back, nothing will!'

Nelly knew a good idea when she heard one and this was a good idea. In fact, it was better than a good idea, it was a Champion of Champions idea!

'Where do the Grerks keep their gog food?' asked Grit.

'Up there,' Nelly pointed.

Grit opened the cupboard and ran a hairy
Huffaluk paw along the top shelf. 'Up where?'
he growled.

Nelly clasped her hands to her head.
'Change of plan,' she groaned. 'We're all out
of gog food.

'Bow, collar and alligator chunks, that's what the Grerks have gone to buy,' sighed Nelly. 'Now what are we going to do?'

Mump and Grit opened all the remaining cupboard doors but found nothing in the same smelly league as a tin of alligator chunks.

'We'll just have to search every front and back garden in the street,' slurped Mump.

'Or the whole estate,' growled Grit.

'We've only got thirty-four minutes to find him!' sighed Nelly.

'Then there is no time to waste!' slurped Mump. 'I'll do the odd house numbers, and you do the even house numbers, Grit. Nelly, you stay here in case Glug comes home!'

A plan was a plan.

'GO GO GO!!!'

All Nelly could do now was pace and pace and wait and hope.

And pace.

And pace.

From the kitchen to the hallway.

From the hallway to the front room.

From the front room back to the kitchen, however she paced and wherever she paced the guilt of losing Gluggy weighed heavily on her shoulders.

'I've lost a gog,' she murmured to herself, 'a Champion of Champions prize-winning gog.'

More pacing took her from the kitchen and out into the back garden. Back into the kitchen, back into the hallway, out through the open front door and right up to the hinges of the Grerks' front gate.

But Gluggy was nowhere to be seen.

'I'd give anything to be covered in gog slobber right now,' she sighed, returning to the house, finally giving the soles of her trainers a break and easing herself back up on to the kitchen counter. 'He'll never come home,' she sighed, removing the gog bowl from the drainer and drying it with a tea towel. 'He's had his dinner, why *should* he come home?'

Why indeed, she might ask.

But come home he most certainly did!

'GLUGGY!' she gasped, as the sound of scrabbling claws colliding with a pasting table became a crescendo of hairy wallpaper rolls tumbling in all directions.

'YOU'RE BACK!' she cheered as Gluggy-wug tornadoed into the kitchen, skated under her feet and disappeared into the cupboard beneath her.

'HE'S BACK!' growled Grit, careering into the kitchen, hot on Glug's tails.

'WE'RE BACK!' slurped Mump with a suckery thwuck. 'We spotted him from the top of the road!'

'He was jumping over garden fences like a race horse!' growled Grit.

'Where's he gone?' squeaked Mump with a breathless thwuckthwuckthwuck.

Nelly crouched down by the cupboard under the sink and made calm reassuring noises in Glug's direction. Glug cowered out of sight with all five tails between his legs. He was a no-show show gog now.

'Oh look, he's hurt his nose,' Nelly said, peering tenderly into the cupboard. Grit and Mump stooped low to inspect the damage. 'I wonder what happened to him?'

'It's only a scratch,' growled Grit.

'It's not even a scratch,' thwucked Mump.

'Who did that to your nose, Glug?' said Nelly gently. 'It's all right, you can come out now. You're home where you belong and Mummy and Daddy will soon be home too, with a nice new bow and collar for you to wear to tomorrow's show.'

'I'll shut the front door in case he tries to run off again,' growled Grit.

'I'll tidy up the hallway,' thwucked Mump.

'Good idea,' said Nelly.

Mump and Grit left Nelly to coax Glug out of the cupboard. When they returned to the kitchen they found Nelly with her head in her hands.

'What's wrong?' slurped Mump.

'Everything!' groaned Nelly. 'Look at his coat!'

Grit's solitary eyeball periscoped forward on its long dangly stalk and inspected Glug's coat at close range.

It was teeming, it was wriggling, it was completely alive with …

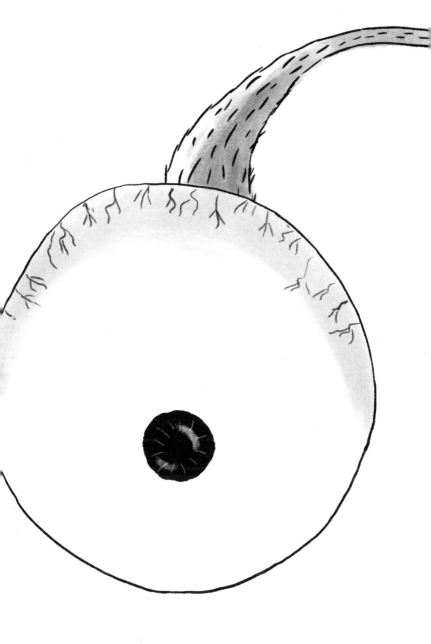

'Oh dear,' growled Grit. 'He's been sniffing around the mingerel at number 252.'

'What's a mingerel?' asked Nelly.

'It's like a mongrel, only more mingin',' explained Mump. 'A lot more mingin', actually.'

Nelly gulped. She'd never seen fleas like them. They were as big as Maltesers, as spiky as hedgehogs, as bouncy as superballs and there were millions of them!

'We've only got twelve minutes to get rid of them!' cried Nelly, watching in amazement as Glug scratched his hind quarters with four back legs at once.

'Run the bath, fetch the soap!' roared Grit, picking Glug up in his blue furry arms and carrying him up the stairs to the bathroom. 'If there's one thing gog fleas hate, Nelly, it's soap!'

Nelly and Mump followed Grit hurriedly up the stairs. There was no time to lose. Nelly emptied a gallon drum of bubble bath into the biggest bath she'd ever seen while Mump turned on the taps and rammed in the plug.

'Bath time!' she slurped. 'Get ready to lower him in!'

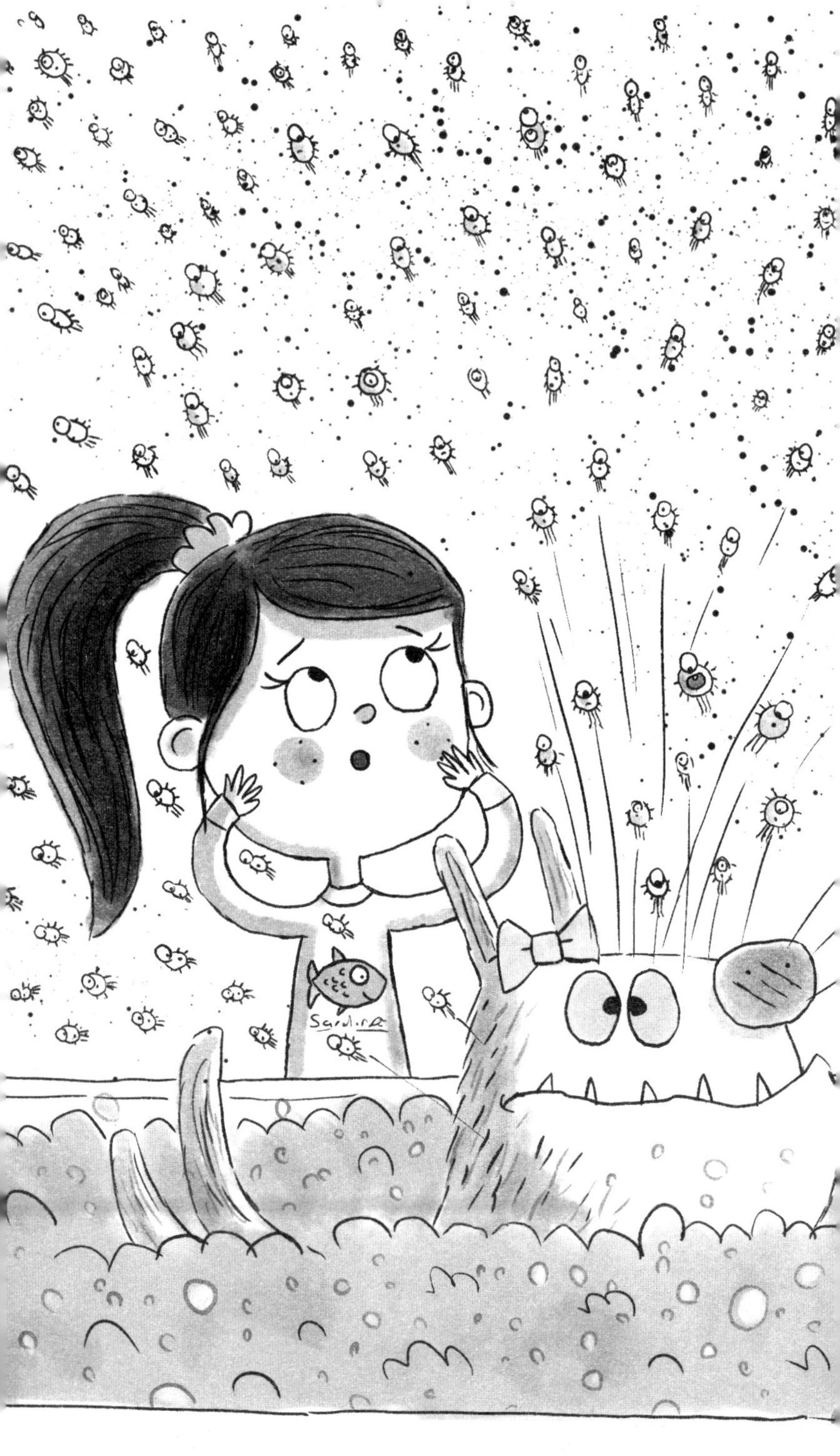

'OUCH!' squeaked Nelly, wheeling round
to protect her face as gog fleas exploded like
gunpowder from Glug's coat.

'It's worked, Grit! It's worked, Mump!
The moment they see the soap, they jump!'
cheered Nelly.

'They're stuck to the ceiling and walls!'
thwucked Mump, waving her tentacles in
all directions.

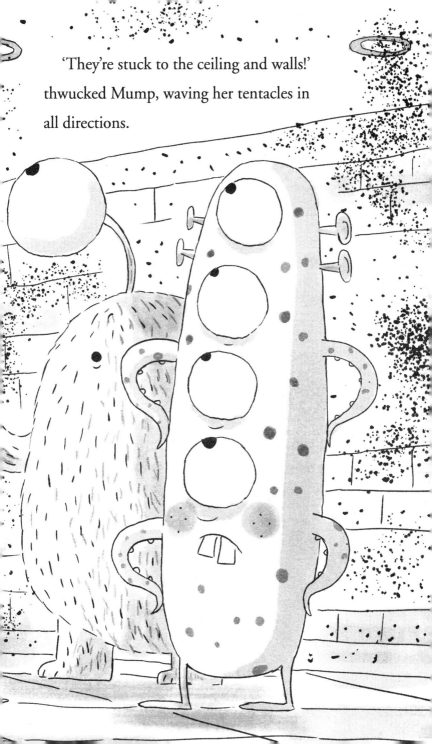

Grit smiled and heaved Glug from the bath, completely free of fleas.

'Look out!' cried Nelly, shielding her eyes. 'They're jumping back!'

It was true. The instant that Glug was lifted from the bath, the gog fleas leapt back on to his coat!

'Put him back in!' thwucked Mump.

Grit duly obliged and once again the gog fleas exploded from his coat.

'Take him back out!' cried Nelly. 'Put him back in! Take him back out!'

Grit dutifully yo-yoed Glug in and out of the bath water but the results were the same every time.

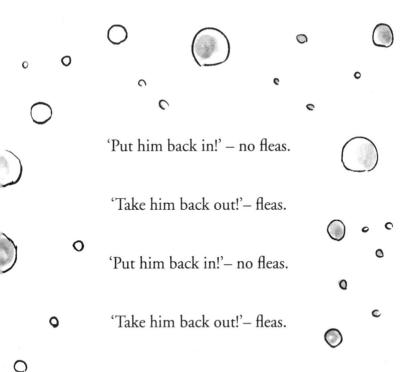

'Put him back in!' – no fleas.

'Take him back out!'– fleas.

'Put him back in!'– no fleas.

'Take him back out!'– fleas.

It was hopeless. Out of the bath, away
from the soap suds, Glug was an unstoppable
flea magnet.

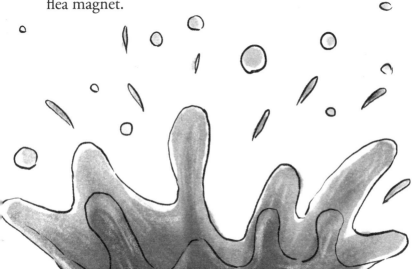

'Carry him into the garden!' thwucked
Mump. 'We can hose him down with soapy
water outside!'

Grit tumbled down the stairs with
flea-ridden Glug in his paws. Nelly and
Mump raced behind them.

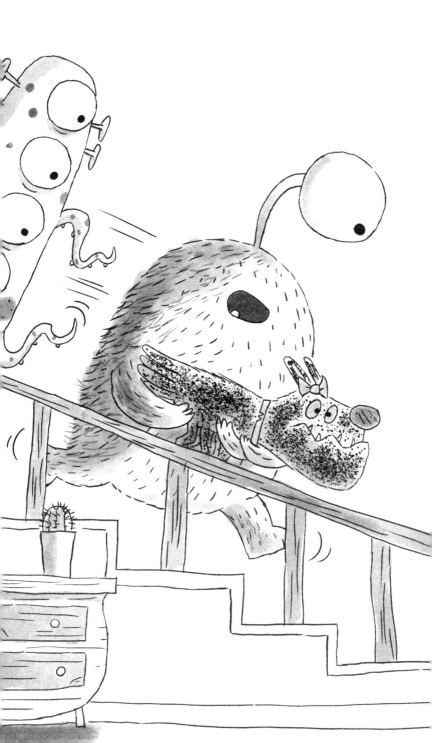

'Get ready with the shampoo,' growled Grit, placing Glug in the middle of the lawn.

Once again the gog fleas exploded from Glug's coat, this time gaining refuge in the surrounding trees and shrubs.

But just as before, they imploded back
on to him the moment Glug had shaken
himself down.

Grit shook his head and growled, Mump closed all four eyes and sucker thwucked. Nelly leapt into the air and whooped!

'Quickquickquick!' she cried, 'I've got an idea! Bring Glug into the lounge, we're going to do some decorating!'

Grit and Mump didn't ask questions. There was far too little time for questions.

With a genius new idea crackling through her brain, Nelly ran through the kitchen, grabbing a bottle of washing-up liquid on the way. 'We need a better bucket, the turquoise one's no use, try and find a bigger empty bucket, THE BIGGER THE BETTER!'

Grit handed Glug to Mump, ran outside into the back garden and came back with a wheelie bin under one of his arms.

'Perfect!' said Nelly, racing into the lounge and pushing the silver-foiled furniture into the middle of the room. She looked at her watch. The Grerks would be home in 6 and a half minutes!

'OK,' said Nelly, 'We need to mix lots of wallpaper paste, and fast!'

Mump handed Glug back to Grit and took charge. With a flurry of tentacles she ripped open six packets of Monsta-Paste, poured them into the wheelie bin, added water and stirred the mixture into a green slimy slop.

I wish I had tentacles, thought Nelly, handing out paste brushes and paint rollers as quickly as she could. 'I need the ceiling and walls pasted from top to bottom, quick as quickquickquick!' she pleaded.

Grit handed Glug to Mump, Mump handed Glug back to Grit, Grit turned to Nelly and decided it was high time he put Glug back down on the floor.

All nine hands set to work. 'Four minutes!' warned Nelly as a blur of orange tentacles and blue furry paws slapped green sloppy goo across the walls and above her head.

'You've missed a bit,' thwucked Mump, throwing a four-eyed perfectionist glance at Grit.

'Never mind that!' shouted Nelly, raising the bottle of washing-up liquid and aiming it directly at Glug.

'Cover your eyes!' she shouted. 'It's soap time again!'

Grit and Mump lowered their pasting brushes and braced themselves for the next flea explosion.

'TAKE THAT!'

smiled Nelly, squeezing hard and then jumping back as the longer-lasting lemon-fresh formula spurted all over Glug's coat.

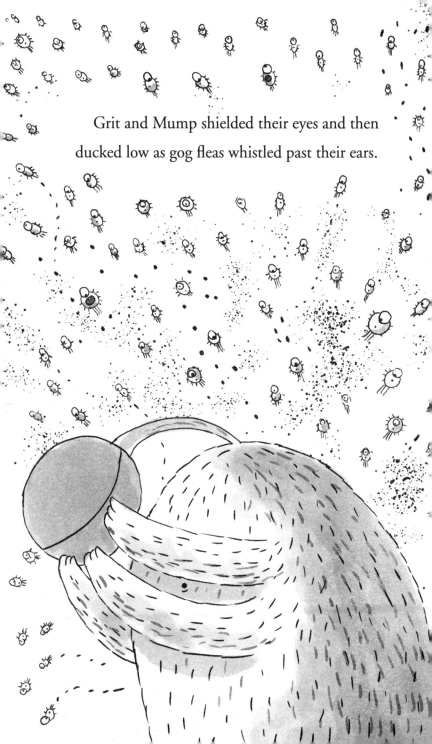

Grit and Mump shielded their eyes and then ducked low as gog fleas whistled past their ears.

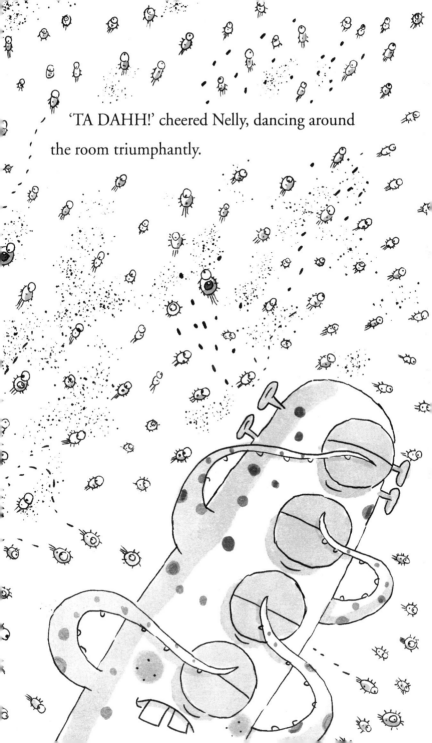

'TA DAHH!' cheered Nelly, dancing around
the room triumphantly.

Nelly had every right to feel pleased with herself.

With just three and a half minutes to spare, her lemon-fresh attack had sent the gog fleas exploding from Glug's coat and clinging to the ceiling and walls of the Grerks' lounge. Only this time that's precisely where they stayed, welded into place by the quick-drying Monsta-Paste!

'Monsta-Paste saves the day!' cheered Nelly, doing a victory jig in the middle of the floor and then remembering there was still more work to do.

'Only we're not finished yet!' she added, handing out large tins of yellow and black spotty paint. 'Ceiling and walls painted in double-quick time please!'

Grit and Mump set to with as many brushes as they could manage. Nelly got busy with the hairdryer, drying and buffing Glug's coat back to tip-top show gog condition.

'Good as new!' she smiled, waving the hairdryer through his bow once more and leaning back to admire the results. He looked perfect. A true Champion of Champions. Apart perhaps from that little mark on his nose.

'Can I borrow your paint tin a minute please, Grit?' Nelly asked.

'I haven't missed a bit, have I?' he growled.

Nelly laughed and shook her head. 'No, but I have!'

Grit and Mump watched as Nelly placed the tip of her index finger into the middle of an oily black circle of paint and then carefully dabbed it on to the tip of Glug's nose.

'Perfect, Gluggy,' she smiled. 'No one would ever know!'

'We're done!' growled Grit triumphantly. 'Do you want us to wash the brushes?'

'There isn't time!' laughed Nelly. 'I want you to run down the garden path as fast as you can and disappear before the Grerks come home!'

It was fifty-four seconds to eight.

'Consider us gone, Nelly!'
slurped Mump with
a suckery thwuck.

'MIND THE BUCKET AND THANKS FOR YOUR HELP!'

shouted Nelly.

Mump and Grit raced out of the house as fast as they had raced in. Although this time taking especially good care to close the front door behind them.

Nelly flopped on to the silver foil covering the sofa and was enthusiastically joined by Glug.

Apart from the scratch on his nose, Glug didn't seem any the worse for his experience at all. In fact, he seemed to be enjoying all the extra fuss. His tongues were just as licky and his tails were just as waggy and due to some very quick thinking on Nelly's part, his coat was now completely flea-free.

'Are you pleased to be home, Gluggy?' she whispered. 'I wish you could tell me where you've been.'

It was a mystery where Glug had escaped to or why he had suddenly run home, but with time ticking by fast, Nelly was just pleased that he had.

With a puff of her cheeks and a slump of her shoulders, she gazed around at the newly decorated ceiling and walls.

'I hope they like it,' she sighed, with an anxious nibble of her lip.

When the Grerks came home, they didn't like it. They loved it!

'I thought we'd go spiky wriggly in here,' said Nelly, pointing to the curious texture of the ceiling and walls.

'How original! How unusual! How creative, Nelly!' squawked Pummice. 'We really are most impressed.'

Scroot peered a little closer. 'Are all my eyes deceiving me, Nelly, or are the yellow and black spots actually wriggling?'

'It does sort of give that effect, yes,' nodded Nelly.

'And you've shampooed Glug as well! How kind!' cried Pummice. 'He's all ready for tomorrow's show! You really didn't have to do that as well!'

'Oh I did, believe me I really did,' smiled Nelly.

Nelly stayed a few extra minutes at number 55 to see Glug crowned with his sparkling new silver collar and topped off with his new golden bow.

Three shakes of a Squiddl's belly button later, she was closing the garden gate and heading back along Sweetman Street in the direction of home.

'YOU'RE AN INTERIOR DESIGN GENIUS, NELLY!'

squawked Pummice and Scroot, waving their tentacles vigorously from the door.

Nelly turned and waved back.

'THAT'S ME!' she laughed, raising a tin of yellow and black spotty paint above her head.

166

'Thanks for this! I'll redecorate my bedroom soon!'

'You're very welcome!' squawked the Grerks. 'If you need any more, let us know.'

Nelly breathed a huge sigh of relief and turned for home.

'That was a very very VERY close call!' she sighed.

CHAPTER

Whenever Nelly returned home from her crazy, heart-stopping monster-sitting adventures, there was always a moment of readjustment. It was like stepping off a fairground waltzer and suddenly being rocked by the steadiness of the ground beneath her. The walls, the furniture, her family's voices, the sounds of the television … everything about number 119 was so quietly and reassuringly normal. Even after the funniest, gunkiest, loopiest, gloopiest monster-sitting adventures, Nelly was never sorry to be home.

This evening, she had her favourite pizza combo to look forward to. Would it be a thin crust? Or would it be deep pan?

It would be chaos.

Utter chaos reigned in the Morton family kitchen that evening because Asti had gone off on one. She was hysterical. Out of control. Stamping her feet and waving her arms as only Asti could.

'I DID SEE IT!!' she was screaming.

'I DID I DID I DID!!!'

Nelly's mum and dad were trying to calm Asti down with a slice of Caribbean pizza with extra pineapple. But the more they waved it in front of her face, the angrier she got.

'IT JUMPED STRAIGHT OVER OUR FENCE, RIGHT OVER NEXT DOOR'S HEDGE. IT WAS HUGE! IT WAS HIDEOUS!!'

Nelly left her American Hot in its box for a moment and listened intently to Asti's outburst. After all, it wasn't often that her sister had something interesting to say.

Asti, sensing a potential ally, shared her frustration with Nelly.

'Nelly, I bet you know what it was. It's probably one of your revolting friends. It had ten legs at least and it must have been the size of a rhinoceros,' she exaggerated.

Nelly looked at her mum. Her mum looked at her dad. Everyone looked at the Caribbean pizza slice.

'I'M TELLING YOU IT WAS STANDING OUT THERE IN THE GARDEN OVER BY THE RABBIT HUTCH!' shrieked Asti. 'IT HAD TWO ORANGE TONGUES, AT LEAST TEN TAILS AND ITS FACE WAS PRESSED RIGHT UP CLOSE TO THE WIRE!! … AND AND … AND IT HAD A BLUE RIBBON ON ITS HEAD!!

'YOU MUST KNOW WHAT IT WAS, NELLY!!' shrieked Asti. 'YOU MUST!!'

Nelly sank her teeth through a hot chilli and

shook her head slowly. 'Are you sure it wasn't a badger?' she asked with a straight face.

'A BADGER?' squealed Asti. 'BADGERS DON'T JUMP FENCES! BADGERS CAN'T HOWL LIKE A PACK OF WOLVES!!'

'A fox, then?' suggested Nelly helpfully.

Asti exploded, slapping the Caribbean pizza slice out of her mum's hand, banging the box on the kitchen counter and stomping upstairs to her room.

Nelly's dad opened Asti's pizza box, picked out all the bits of ham and added them to his Meat Feast.

'How were the Grerks? Did you have a nice time, love?'

'I had a lovely time, thanks,' said Nelly thoughtfully.

Later that evening, before retiring to her room to write her notes, Nelly offered to put the empty pizza boxes in the recycling bin outside. On the short trip back across the patio, she stopped to talk to a friend.

'Hello, beautiful,' she whispered. 'Do you know something I don't know?'

Snowball took time out from a cabbage leaf, hopped across the hutch and pressed his soft pink nose against the wire wall of his cage.

'You didn't by any chance meet a gog called Glug today, did you? And you didn't by any chance nip him on the nose, did you? And you're not by any chance the reason that Glug ran all the way home to me, are you, Snowball?'

Snowball flopped his ears to one side and stared indifferently through the wire.

'I owe you, Snowball,' whispered Nelly.

LOOK OUT FOR THE NEXT

NELLY THE MONSTER SITTER

BOOK

THE SQUURMS AT NO. 322